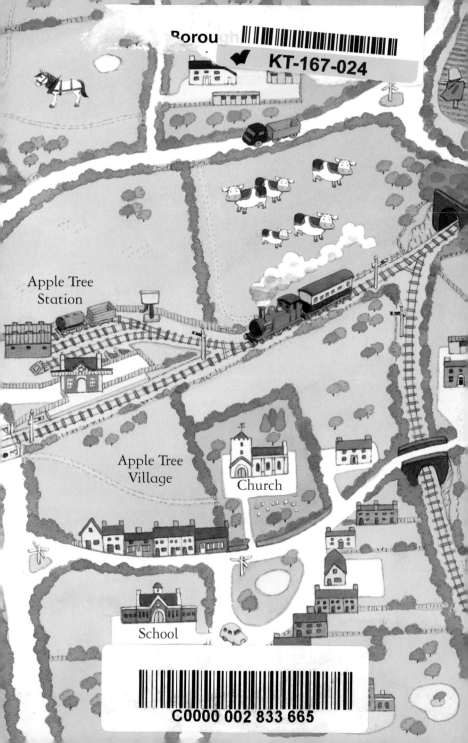

Borough

Apple Tree
Station

Apple Tree
Village

Church

School

Farmyard Tales

The Snow Storm

Heather Amery

Illustrated by Stephen Cartwright

Adapted by Lara Bryan
Reading consultant: Alison Kelly

Find the duck on every double page.

This story is about
Apple Tree Farm,

Sam,

Poppy,

Mrs. Boot,

Ted,

Rusty,

and
Woolly.

One morning, Poppy,
Sam and Mrs. Boot
looked out of the door.

Gosh!

In the night, there had been a snow storm.

Poppy and Sam went
out to play.

Ted walked past with
a sleigh full of hay.

7

"Thank you for pulling the hay," said Ted.

"It's for the sheep."

"Where are all the
sheep?" asked Sam.

"They're covered in snow!" said Ted.

They brushed the snow
off the sheep and gave
them lots of hay.

Poppy counted the sheep.

"Woolly is missing!"
she said.

They looked around the snowy field.

Rusty ran towards
the hedge.

"Rusty's found
something," said Sam.

Ted looked under
the hedge.

"There's Woolly!"
Poppy cried.

"Out you come,
Woolly," said Ted.

"Clever Rusty,"
said Poppy.

"There's something else in there," Sam cried.

Ted lifted out
a tiny lamb.

"Woolly's had a baby,"
Ted said.

They took Woolly and
her lamb to the barn.

"You'll be warm soon,"
said Poppy.

What a snowy
surprise!

PUZZLES

Puzzle 1

Put the five pictures in the right order.

A.

B.

C.

D.

E.

Puzzle 2

Can you help Poppy count the number of:

    sheep   hats   rabbits

Puzzle 3

Spot five differences between these two pictures.

Puzzle 4

Which sentence goes with each picture?

A.

It was raining!
It was snowing!

B.

Poppy made a snowman.
Poppy made a scarecrow.

C.

They pushed the hay.
They pulled the hay.

D.

They looked around.
They ran around.

Answers to puzzles
Puzzle 1

1B.

2C.

3E.

4D.

5A.

Puzzle 2

There are <u>six</u> sheep, <u>three</u> hats and <u>two</u> rabbits.

Puzzle 3

Puzzle 4

A. It was snowing!

B. Poppy made a snowman.

C. They pulled the hay.

D. They looked around.

Designed by Laura Nelson
Digital manipulation by Nick Wakeford

This edition first published in 2017 by Usborne Publishing Ltd.,
Usborne House, 83-85 Saffron Hill, London EC1N 8RT, England.
www.usborne.com Copyright © 2017, 1994 Usborne Publishing Ltd.

USBORNE FIRST READING
Level Two Farmyard Tales

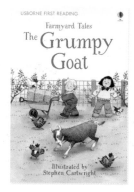

USBORNE FIRST READING
Farmyard Tales
The **Grumpy Goat**
Illustrated by Stephen Cartwright

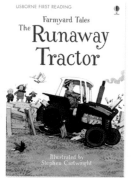

USBORNE FIRST READING
Farmyard Tales
The **Runaway Tractor**
Illustrated by Stephen Cartwright

USBORNE FIRST READING
Farmyard Tales
The **Naughty Sheep**
Illustrated by Stephen Cartwright

USBORNE FIRST READING
Farmyard Tales
Tractor in Trouble
Illustrated by Stephen Cartwright

USBORNE FIRST READING
Farmyard Tales
Scarecrow's Secret
Illustrated by Stephen Cartwright

USBORNE FIRST READING
Farmyard Tales
Surprise Visitors
Illustrated by Stephen Cartwright

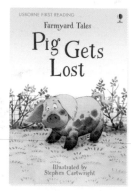

USBORNE FIRST READING
Farmyard Tales
Pig Gets Lost
Illustrated by Stephen Cartwright

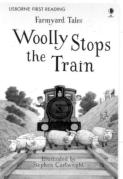

USBORNE FIRST READING
Farmyard Tales
Woolly Stops the Train
Illustrated by Stephen Cartwright

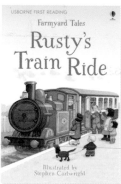

USBORNE FIRST READING
Farmyard Tales
Rusty's Train Ride
Illustrated by Stephen Cartwright